KT-163-101

Hare was dozing in the sun
when he saw Tortoise walk past.
At once, Hare was alert and angry.
The last time Hare had met Tortoise
was when that slowpoke had beaten him
in a race. Hare was still embarrassed.

3

Hare called, "Tortoise! Hey, Tortoise!"
He hopped over and said,
"Do you want to have another race?"

Tortoise stared at him. "All right.
Will you have a nap like last time?"

That made Hare furious.
"This time I will beat you!"
he bellowed.

4

Tortoise and Hare

Written by Ye-shil Kim
Illustrated by Rashin Kheiriyeh
Edited by Joy Cowley

Windsor and Maidenhead

95800000037670

Yawn!

2

"Get set! Go!"

The second race began.
Hare hopped very fast.
Tortoise crawled and crawled.

When Hare looked back,
he saw Tortoise was far behind.
But Hare was not taking any chances.

7

Nearby, a monkey was eating a banana.
Hare grabbed the banana peel
and threw it in front of Tortoise.

When Tortoise stepped on the banana peel,
he slipped and flipped over onto his back.

Hare ran back into the race.

10

Hare was feeling hot.
When he saw the ice-cream cart,
he stopped and bought
a delicious ice-cream treat.
He was so busy eating
and talking to his friends
that he forgot about the race.
But what was this?
Tortoise was crawling past.

Hare could not believe it!
He ran and ran to pass Tortoise.

Hare thought he would
put Tortoise out of the race.
He got a shovel and dug a deep hole.
Then he covered the hole with sticks.
Tortoise would fall in the hole
and be stuck. Ha ha!

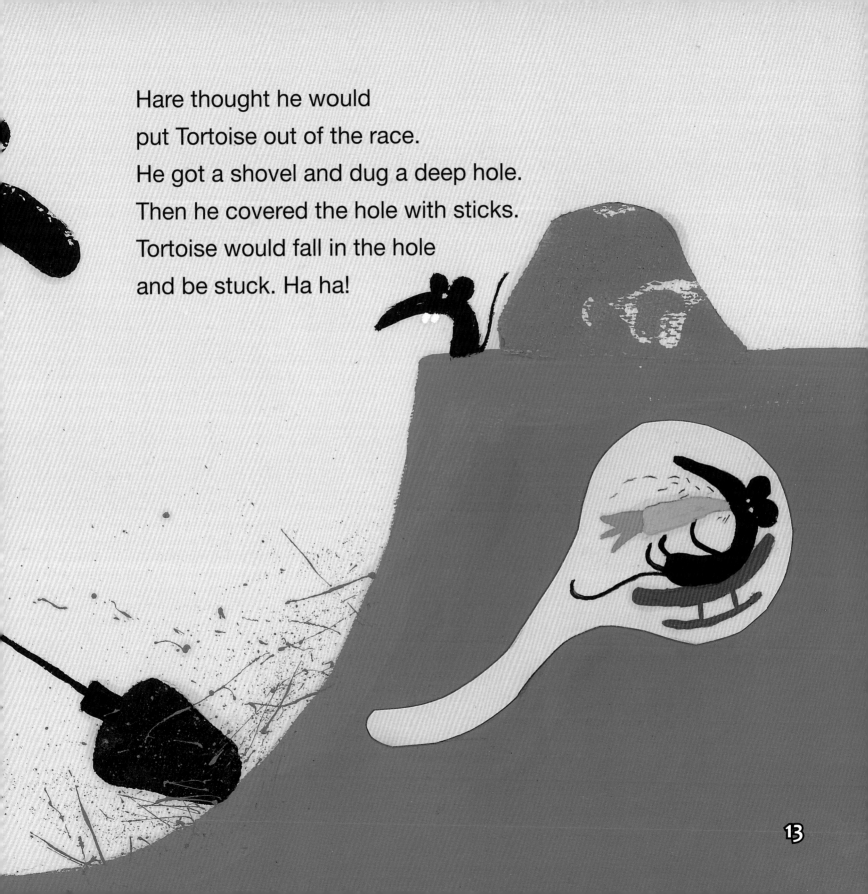

Sure enough,
Tortoise fell in the hole.
Hare laughed and laughed.
Tortoise couldn't get out of the hole.
Now Hare would win the race for sure.

Ouch!

Hare was not in a hurry
to get to the finish line.
He met up with his friends
and played some games.
But wait! A surprise!
Tortoise was crawling past.
That was impossible!
How did he get out of the hole?

16

Hare was very annoyed.
He put a sign on the road that said:
ROAD CLOSED. DETOUR.
The sign pointed to a path
that went far away
from the finish line.

ROAD CLOSED.
DETOUR.

ROAD CLOSED.
DETOUR.

Tortoise looked at the sign
and then went down the path.

Hare watched him go.
"I won't waste time," said Hare.
"Now I'll run to the finish line."

But something amazing happened.
As Hare ran towards the finish line,
slowpoke Tortoise crawled over it.
"No!" cried Hare. "No, no, no!"

This is what happened.
When Tortoise slipped
on the banana peel,
the monkey helped him.

Tortoise went on with the race.

The tortoise who passed
the ice-cream cart
and then fell in the hole
was one of Tortoise's brothers.

Tortoise went on with the race.

23

The tortoise who passed Hare
playing games with his friends
was the tortoise who went
down the wrong path.
He was Tortoise's other brother!

Meanwhile, Tortoise went on with the race.

24

Slowly but surely,
Tortoise won the race.

Hare kicked his feet and cried.
"How did you do it?
Tortoise, how did you win?"

"Hare, don't cry," said Tortoise.
"It's not important who wins or loses,
only that you do your best!
Everyone knows you are the fastest.
If you had played fair, you would have won."
Then Tortoise went to find his brothers.

Hare was so ashamed,
he could not lift his head.
The next time, he would play fair.

Dear Tortoise,

Everyone knows you are slow, but I was beaten by you
two times! I was embarrassed and ashamed.

Now I need to thank you because you taught me a lesson.
I have always been scared of losing, but I learned
there is something more important than winning.
I need to be honest and fair, and do the best I can.
If you will agree to a third race with me,
I promise to play fair.

Your friend, Hare

big & SMALL

Original Korean text by Ye-shil Kim
Illustrations by Rashin Kheiriyeh
Original Korean edition © Eenbook 2011

This English edition published by Big & Small in 2015
by arrangement with Eenbook
English text edited by Joy Cowley
Additional editing by Mary Lindeen
Artwork for this edition produced
in cooperation with Norwood House Press, USA
English edition © Big & Small 2015

All rights reserved

ISBN: 978-1-925234-00-8

Printed in Korea